Let's Eat Weeds!

Annie Raser-Rowland
and Adam Grubb

A kids' guide to foraging

Illustrations by Evie Barrow

SCRIBBLE

No guide to foraging can provide exhaustive safety information, including this one. Common sense and further research are recommended. Your safety is your responsibility and no liability is accepted for injury incurred while using this book as a reference.

CONTENTS

INTRODUCTION

Did you know that every time you go for a walk in the park and you step on a plant, you could be walking on someone's lunch? By 'someone' we don't mean bugs, worms, birds, and wombats — although they might like to eat some of it too. We mean the lunch of *actual human beings*. It turns out that there's free food growing everywhere! Not many people even know about this. They don't notice that all around them are plants you can turn into soups, salads, and sandwiches! We (that is, the authors of this here book) know a lot about it though, and after much discussion we've decided that we're going to let *you* in on the secret. We guess we're just very nice people like that.

First let's imagine something — but we'll be imagining something that was *real*. Once upon a time there was no Woolies, no Coles — in fact, there were no shops at all. There weren't even any farms. The way people got food was to go *looking* for it. Some of the 'food' had legs and they had to chase it. But we're not going to talk about that! We'll stick to talking about some of the wild *plants* they ate. Because many of these plants still live among us.

Not all plants are the same, of course. There are the ones we buy and then plant in the ground exactly where we want them to grow. But other plants start growing without us doing anything at all. Some of these

plants are from Australia, and some come from other places. Their tiny seeds get blown in the wind or sometimes delivered by birds. (When birds deliver plants they don't use envelopes. They eat berries and then they poo out the seeds. Yes, that's how *birds* deliver things—luckily, birds don't run the post office.) So anyway, all these plants start growing where we didn't put them. Some people get a bit angry about this, and they call these wild plants 'weeds'.

Most plants are definitely not edible. You should never, ever taste a random plant that you don't know. But for some weird reason, most 'weeds' *are* edible. There are weeds that don't taste very good and also a few that are poisonous. But others are yum!

So let's learn about some weeds you can eat! But first, the beginning of this book is going to be about how to be very, very careful when you are harvesting wild plants. Then we're going to talk about eight plants that are pretty easy to get to know. Once you've learnt to identify at least three of them, you'll have earned your 'Advanced Forager's Licence'. Then—and only then—you should learn about the other seven plants, because they are a little bit trickier.

Are you ready? Let's go!

HOW TO BE VERY, VERY CAREFUL

Know Your Plant

There are plants you wouldn't want to eat because they are made of wood, or covered in prickles, or just taste plain awful. And then, of course, some plants are poisonous. Since we're not living in a fairytale, if you do eat a poisonous plant you don't just fall into a deep, deep sleep for a year until a frog wakes you up by kissing you. No, these plants can make you very, very sick.

Some poisonous plants can look a little bit like some edible plants. You can learn to spot the differences between them pretty easily. But you do have to learn!

Both the words and illustrations in this book are important in helping you to learn. The easiest plants to identify and harvest safely are in the first half of the book. Take it slowly — don't go out eating them all on your first day foraging! Choose one or two of the 'easy weeds' to learn about first. Once you're sure about those ones, you can move on to a new weed.

ALWAYS make sure you have the right plant before you eat it. If you are even a tiny bit unsure, then DON'T EAT IT!

On our website, letseatweeds.com, you'll find extra photos to look at and quizzes you can do. Can you match the weeds in this book to their photos and tell them apart from any look-alike plants? Find out!

Allergies

Everyone's body is different. You probably know a kid who can't drink milk without getting a bellyache, whereas another kid you know can drink three chocolate milkshakes in a row and feel just perfect. So when you first start eating wild plants, start small and see how your body responds; go for a sandwich with a handful of weeds hanging out with the cheese and tomato, rather than a bowl of weed salad bigger than your head. If you know that you have an intolerance to tomatoes, eggplants, and capsicums, skip eating blackberry nightshade (page 58), because it belongs to the same plant family.

Poisons in the Environment

Unfortunately, soils sometimes have poisons in them. These can come from old paint, the smoke from factories and cars, and some old chemicals people used to kill insects with. Plants are usually fairly good at keeping the poisons out of their leaves and fruit. But you should avoid eating plants from anywhere you think might have poisons in the ground. And always wash any food grown in the city, including weeds.

The sprays used to kill weeds aren't good for you either. Sometimes the people who manage the parks use coloured herbicide and put up signs to let you know when weeds have been sprayed. But a lot of times they don't. For this reason the safest weeds are the ones from your own backyard.

Poop

We're sure that you mastered the art of not eating poop back when you were two years old. But we have to say it: always check that an animal hasn't done its business on a plant that you're about to eat. Wee, of course, is invisible — another good reason to wash your weeds…

Cooking

Some of the recipes in this book involve using knives, blenders, and very hot stoves. In a restaurant kitchen the head chefs are the bosses, and they don't do a lot of cutting, blending, and cooking. The people called cooks do most of that! So if you're not confident yet using knives and stoves, we suggest that you take the part of the head chef and ask an adult to be your cook.

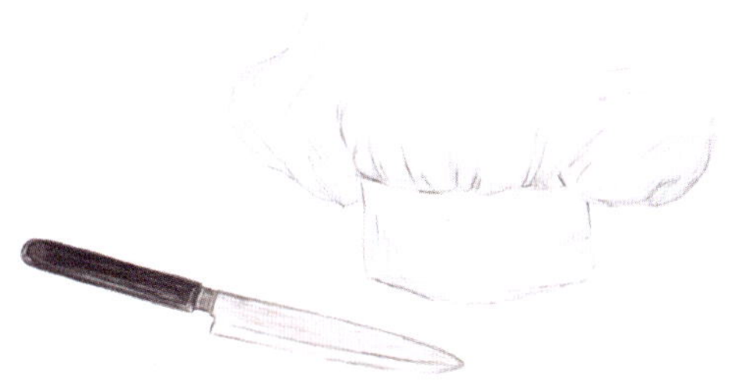

Oxalic Acid

Oxalic acid is a natural plant chemical found in many common foods. Bananas, spinach, parsley, almonds, chocolate, and tea all contain quite a lot of it. So do a handful of the plants in this book. Eating too much oxalic acid can reduce how well your body uses an important mineral called calcium. The good news is that leafy green vegetables — especially weeds — contain quite high levels of calcium themselves. It can still be good to eat your high-oxalic-acid foods at the same time as other high-calcium foods like milk, yoghurt, and cheese. You can also blanch the food in boiling water to remove the oxalic acid and then throw the water away (probably don't try this with chocolate!).

A NOTE FOR GROWN-UPS

Dear reader, if you are not an adult, please show this part of the book to one of the grown-ups who takes care of you. We'll give you a minute… Great. Thank you.

Dear grown-ups, if you would like to know more, there are resources available for teachers, carers, and parents on our website letseatweeds.com. They include plant photographs and more information on some of the risks mentioned in the previous chapter. If you are looking for a book for adults, we can humbly recommend our book *The Weed Forager's Handbook: A Guide to Edible and Medicinal Weeds in Australia.*

If you feel like you need further help identifying any of the plants in this book there are online communities, including the Facebook group 'Edible Weeds, Wild Plants & Foraging in Australia', where you can upload images for assistance.

Because this book is written for kids, we haven't included cautions related to adult concerns such as arthritis or pregnancy. If you are pregnant or trying to conceive you should limit your consumption of a couple of plants — notably oxalis and blackberry nightshade.

Every plant in this book has been eaten by millions of people around the world for thousands of years. Our goal is to give kids agency to interact with the outside world and learn skills that allow them to meaningfully add to their diet, while not risking their health. To that end we've been meticulous about researching the safety of each plant. If you have any questions we're happy to take your enquiries at info@letseatweeds.com.

HOW TO BE VERY, VERY GOOD AT PICKING AND PREPARING WEEDS

If a lettuce you buy from a shop is like a tame cat, then edible weeds are like tigers. And, just as with tigers, it helps if you know how to handle them. Here are some tips:

1) When you are picking your weeds, choose plants that look lush and healthy. Really straggly weeds with lots of insect damage often have leathery leaves that aren't so nice to eat.

2) Pick the young growth of the plant. These leaves and shoots look fresher and brighter green than the older growth. In many plants the youngest growth is towards the end of each stalk or stem. The young growth is the softest part of the plant and has a gentler flavour, so it's especially good to focus your picking on these parts if you're making a salad. Look for the dashed line on the plant pictures for some ideas about where to pick.

3) Chop your weeds across the grain. This means chopping across the stalks, stems, and the veins in the leaves. Some weeds have chewier textures than vegetables from a shop, so chopping them up like this stops you from getting stringy bits stuck in your teeth.

Meet **Real-Size Bee**. Why does he have such a weird name? Well, because he helps you to understand the real size of the plants in the drawings in this book. You'll find him buzzing about in lots of the pictures you're about to see.

As well as Real-Size Bee, we've included this handy ruler in case you want to check the length of any leaves or flowers you find… but have lost your pencil case under a mountain of dirty clothes.

OXALIS

(Scientific name: Oxalis species)

Lots of kids are already in the know about oxalis because of a particular kind that gets called 'sourgrass'. It has a lemon-yellow trumpet-shaped flower and often grows among long grass. When you chew on the flower stalks they taste really sour (in a screwing-your-face-up-but-you-like-it kind of way).

What To Look For

Look down to the bottom of a sourgrass flower stalk and you'll see a clump of leaves. Each leaf stem has three little leaves at its tip. This makes it look a bit like clover, but you can tell the difference because each of clover's leaves are usually oval, whereas oxalis's leaves are shaped like love hearts. (Don't sweat if you get confused and eat clover—it won't taste as nice as oxalis, but it isn't at all poisonous.)

Oxalis leaves can do a pretty good trick: if they don't like what's going on they fold up and take a rest. Too sunny? Too rainy? Too night-time-y? 'Catch you later alligator,' say oxalis leaves.

Sourgrass isn't the only type of oxalis and yellow isn't the only colour oxalis flowers come in. Pink, purple, and white are also popular. The flowers don't always grow on such tall stalks as with sourgrass either: some nestle right down low near the leaves. The flowers always have five petals though, and in some species they turn into long seed capsules covered in miniscule, silky hairs.

Where To Look

Oxalis grows in any of the states of Australia, as long as it can find a moist patch of earth.

When To Look

All year round, though they will pack up and leave town if conditions get too hot and dry for their liking.

How To Pick And Prepare It

You won't need a chainsaw to harvest this little cutie. Simply pluck as many leaves and flowers as you'd like with your fingers. And then double that amount, because your oxalis is about to perform a marvellous disappearing trick: as soon as you cook it, or even chop it up finely, it shrinks like an icicle in a heatwave.

There's a plant called 'lucky clover' that has four instead of three leaves on each stem. Luckily you can eat it, because it's actually a type of oxalis.

How To Use It

It's hard to pick a lot of oxalis. That's not a bad thing, for two reasons:

1) It contains oxalic acid, so you don't want to eat too much at one time (see the information on oxalic acid on page 5).
2) Its flavour is so powerful that it's like being punched in the mouth by a tiny, lemon-flavoured Incredible Hulk.

This second reason is why you should think of oxalis as more of a herb than a vegetable. That lemony punch tastes great in a stir-fry, risotto, omelette, or frittata, or just in cream cheese sandwiches. This last one is fun because you can press the leaves into the cream cheese so that they keep their heart shapes. After you put the lid on your sandwich, *you'll* still know they're in there, even if no one else does.

Once upon a time people used oxalis a lot for making sauces, especially to go with fish. You could make your own version by grinding some leaves up with a little bit of salt and something creamy in a mortar and pestle. Then dunk some homemade potato or sweet potato wedges in it. Pazow!

In South Africa sourgrass is cooked along with meat and other wild plants in a stew called (take a deep breath before trying to say this) *waterblommetjiebredie*.

DANDELION

(Scientific name: Taraxacum species)

The name for dandelion in France is dent-de-lion, *which means 'tooth of the lion'. Have a look at the 'tooth' shapes along the edge of a dandelion's leaves, and you can probably guess why. If you say the French name out loud you might even be able to guess where the word 'dandelion' came from.*

What To Look For

You might already know what dandelion looks like because it is the plant that people sometimes use to make a wish, while blowing away the fluffy ball of seeds. Each seed flies off like a miniature umbrella in the wind.

Besides their lion's-teeth leaves, dandelions also have shaggy, golden-yellow flowers that look a bit like a lion's mane. The leaves all grow right out of the plant's centre, which is at ground level. Every dandelion flower grows on its own hollow stalk. When you pick the flower, white sap forms in a circle on the broken flower stalk.

The flower transforms into that fluffy white ball of seeds, which, if you really, *really* used your imagination, could even be the ghost of a lion floating away into the sky…

Where To Look

You can find dandelion in lawns, you can find it in garden beds, you can find it under trees – you can find it all over the place! It grows in every state in Australia, but prefers the cooler parts of the country.

When To Look

All year round, but the leaves are usually nicest for eating in winter and spring.

How To Pick And Prepare It

If you are planning on eating dandelion raw, pick leaves that are soft and bright green. These often grow towards the centre of the plant. If you are planning on cooking it, you can take older outer leaves. Some people cut the whole plant off at ground level with a knife, but we usually just pluck the leaves off. Because they grow so close to the ground they usually need a really good wash.

To harvest the flower petals, pick the whole flower, then pull the golden petals out from the green base.

How To Use It

Some people like spicy food, some people like sour food, and some people like bitter food. Dandelion is bitter, and not everyone likes that. Many poisonous plants are bitter-tasting. But some plants that are really healthy for you, like dandelion, are bitter too. Bitter plants take some time to get used to, but after a while they can start to taste delicious.

If you learn to like dandelion, then you'll have a lot of free vitamins! It is one of the most vitamin- and mineral-packed plants ever tested by scientists. Young dandelion leaves are really good in sandwiches and salads. If you're using the leaves raw, chop them up so they're easy to chew.

In Greece they boil the leaves in salty

The French actually have two names for dandelion. As well as *dent-de-lion* they also call it *pissenlit*, which means 'wee the bed', because dandelion (like tea) makes you pee a bit more. Don't worry though — we've eaten it hundreds of times and it's never caused us to *pissenlit*. Promise!

water for about 20 minutes, then strain them and serve them with lemon juice and olive oil — this dish is called *horta*. A lot of the bitterness disappears when you cook them this way. *Hortopita* (see recipe on page 38) is when you mix in some feta cheese and eggs, cover it with filo pastry, and bake it into a dandelion pie.

You can also put the petals from the flowers into salads or sprinkle them over any food to make it look fancy. People even dig up the roots and roast them to make a drink a bit like coffee (that one's quite hard work). Our friend Woody, who is eight-and-a-half, picks the hollow flower stalks and uses them as a drinking straw!

The round seed heads of dandelions are sometimes called 'clocks'. The reason behind this is a bit mysterious. Some people say that the number of puffs of breath that it takes to blow all the seeds away can tell you the time — three puffs means it's three o'clock, and so on. We've never tried this ourselves, so please give it a go and if it works, write us a letter so that we can sell our watches.

some examples of different dandelion-leaf shapes

Some people get dandelion confused with a plant called cat's-ears (scientific name: *Hypochaeris* species). Cat's-ears' flowers don't follow dandelion's one-flower-per-stalk rule. Its leaves have rounded and wavy edges (rather than toothed) and are often a bit hairy. You can eat cat's-ears, it's just not as nice as dandelion.

WILD WEEDY SALAD

INGREDIENTS

3 tablespoons mixed sunflower seeds and pumpkin seeds
1 teaspoon tamari or soy sauce
1 red or pink apple
4 tablespoons extra virgin olive oil
2 tablespoons balsamic or apple cider vinegar
Salt and pepper to taste
Enough mixed weeds to fill a large salad bowl
4 tablespoons dandelion and/or angled onion flowers

NOTES

Makes enough for 4 people as a side dish

Because you're using them in a salad, pick the youngest, most tender leaves. Chickweed, dandelion, wild lettuce, sow thistle, and mallow are all wonderful if in season. You can also add a little purslane and finely chopped angled onion.

DIRECTIONS

Toast the seeds (without oil) in a frying pan over a very low heat, stirring occasionally. As they begin to brown, sprinkle them with the tamari. Turn off the heat and keep stirring for a few more seconds. Allow to cool completely.

Chop the apple into thin slices.

Mix the olive oil, vinegar, salt, and pepper in a small jar and shake well.

Remove any large stems from your weeds and wash them well. Pat them dry in a teatowel and chop across the grain.

Put the weeds and the apple slices into your salad bowl and mix in the dressing. Sprinkle the toasted seeds and flower petals over the top immediately before serving.

PURSLANE

(Scientific name: Portulaca oleracea)

The giant Amazonian water lily has leaves so big that you could use one to wrap the tallest person in the world up like a burrito! But the plant we're about to talk about, purslane, is much smaller, and its leaves are only about one or two centimetres long. Despite its size, we prefer purslane because: 1) It's delicious and 2) It's impossible for anyone to turn you into a human burrito with it!

What To Look For

Purslane's little leaves are thick, plump, and juicy. Even the stems are round and juicy. These stems start green when young, but soon turn a reddish colour. Plants like purslane and cactuses, which have leaves or stems that are plump with juices, we call 'succulents'. Usually purslane spreads out very flatly along the ground, with each reddish stem growing out from a central point. There's even a famous Spanish song that goes, '*Es bonita y es bonita, la verdolaga, por el suelo*', which means: 'It's pretty, it's pretty, the purslane growing on the ground.'

When it's growing crowded together with its brothers and sisters, purslane may reach upwards a little towards the sun, sometimes to knee height. (To be clear though, not the knee height of the tallest person in the world. More like a kid's knee height.)

It grows very small yellow flowers with

ripe purslane seed capsules

Purslane is native to much of the world, including Australia. Indigenous people of the central desert would dry it out on kangaroo skins to collect the seeds for making bread.

five petals. These turn into seed capsules that look like pointy gnome hats. When the hats fall off they reveal a green bowl about the right size for a grasshopper's dinner. This bowl is full of tiny round black seeds.

Where To Look

Purslane loves full sun, and it pops up in sunny spots on bare soil, or even out of cracks in concrete. You can find it on every continent in the world except Antarctica, and it grows all over Australia.

When To Look

Purslane loves the hot months, so it doesn't bother showing up until spring. In all but the warmest parts of Australia it completely refuses to come out to play in winter.

How To Pick And Prepare It

Luckily you don't have to pick off all the tiny leaves because the stems of purslane are tasty too. For salads, use your fingers or scissors to harvest the freshest young shoots. As long as they snap off crisply they will be good to eat. You can eat the flowers and seeds too. Older and longer shoots should be cooked. This makes them soften up nicely.

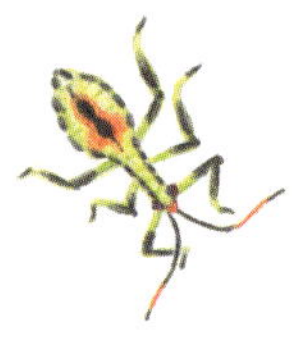

The famous ancient Roman Pliny the Elder believed purslane to be a powerful medicinal plant. He even advised wearing it as an amulet to protect against evil! On the other hand, Pliny liked mixing together things like pigeon poo, the ashes of weasel brains, viper venom, and honey to make 'medicines', so we're not sure how much to trust his advice.

Purslane contains lots of some healthy stuff called 'omega-3 fatty acids'. In fact, it has more than any other plant that grows on land!

How To Use It

Fresh purslane is crunchy and refreshing with a gentle lemony tang. It's totally delicious chopped up finely and mixed with tomato, red onion, olive oil, and salt and pepper. If you're cooking it, you can chop it more roughly. It's great mixed in with an omelette or scrambled eggs. Try it as a side vegetable, or in stews, curries, and pasta sauces. It's a favourite in Mexican food, so wrap it in a tortilla with some beans and salsa to make a burrito.

Purslane is super healthy and full of vitamins. However, like spinach and many other foods, it does contain oxalic acid — check out page 5 for more on this. Already read it? Excellent — then you know that it's good to eat dairy foods at the same time as foods containing oxalic acid. Which is perfect, because purslane is so delicious in a yoghurt dip that we've put a recipe for it on the next page.

PURSLANE YOGHURT DIP (TZATZIKI)

INGREDIENTS

1 cup washed purslane, tightly packed
½ cup good-quality plain yoghurt
2 cloves garlic, crushed
½ teaspoon salt
1 tablespoon extra-virgin olive oil
Flatbread

NOTES

Makes enough for 4 people

DIRECTIONS

Remove the thicker stems from the purslane. Chop it finely.

In a bowl, mix together the yoghurt, garlic, oil, and salt.

Add the purslane to the yoghurt mixture and stir it in.

Put the dip in the refrigerator to chill for at least half an hour, then serve it with fresh or toasted flatbread.

This dip also tastes great on a baked potato, or with falafels or fritters.

MALLOW

(Scientific name: Malva species)

People have been eating mallow for a really, really, really long time—at least 12,000 years, according to archaeologists! A famous poet who lived in Italy 2,000 years ago wrote that he liked to eat mostly olives, mallow, and chicory (another weed!). That poet probably had a very happy tummy, because mallow contains special goo that helps to soothe your insides.

What To Look For

Mallow leaves are big and round with wavy outlines. They look a bit like geranium leaves. If you touch them they feel sort of fuzzy—not smooth like some leaves. If you turn them over, they are lighter green underneath.

There are a few different types of mallow, and their flowers can be pink, purple, white, or somewhere in between. These five-petalled flowers turn into funny seeds that look like little wheels of cheese wrapped in paper—pale-green cheese in fuzzy green paper! Some people even call mallow 'cheese weed'.

Some mallow plants grow only as tall as your knees. Others grow as tall as your head.

Where To Look

Mallow isn't fussy. It will grow in sunny places, wild corners of parks and gardens, dry places, and wet places, in every state of Australia.

When To Look

All year round.

How To Pick And Prepare It

First, make sure your mallow doesn't have 'mallow measles'. This is what we call it when mallow plants get little orange spots all over their leaves. It usually happens when the plant is getting old. Choose fresh, healthy leaves and try not to pick any stem.

Are there some of those miniature 'wheels of cheese' on the plant too? If the cheese is still plump and pale green (it turns brown later), you can pick it.

open-type calyx cheese

mallow measles
closed-type calyx cheese
old dry cheese

How To Use It

In some countries, like Egypt and Lebanon, mallow is called *molokhia*, and people cook it all the time. They make a delicious soup out of mallow leaves, onions, garlic, coriander, stock, lemon juice, and olive oil.

Mallow has a mild flavour that goes with most things. You can eat the youngest leaves raw in a salad, but the other leaves are tastiest if you cook them. We cook them for a long time to let that fuzziness transform into a lovely, soft, schloopy texture. Try making ratatouille with mallow instead of zucchini.

'But what about the cute little cheeses?!' we can hear you yelling. Well, just fry them up with anything like mushrooms and onions and they are yummy as can be.

Hundreds of years ago, people who lived in the area that's now called Germany ate mallow. They also used its stalk fibres to make clothes. They believed this wonderfully useful plant was a gift from their goddess Freyja—who supposedly got around in a flying chariot pulled by cats. Imagine how hard that would be to steer!

A cup of mallow leaves has been found to contain even more calcium than the same amount of milk, and is packed with almost as much protein. Mallow also contains more than twice as much iron as kale.

a small white mallow flower

a big purple mallow flower

Mallow is related to marshmallow, which was used once upon a time to make those soft white treats that you roast around the campfire ... or burn to a sad lump of ash if you forget to watch them for even one second. The scientific name for mallow is *Malva*, which actually comes from an Ancient Greek word meaning 'soft'.

MALLOW & CHICKPEA STEW

INGREDIENTS

5 cups tightly-packed, youngish mallow leaves
1 cup chickpeas (⅔ of a tin)
1½ cups chopped tomatoes (1 tin)
Zest and juice of 1 small lemon
3 cloves garlic, crushed
3 tablespoons chopped dates (or sultanas)
2 teaspoons ground coriander
1 teaspoon ground cumin
1 teaspoon salt
Pepper to taste
2 tablespoons extra virgin olive oil

DIRECTIONS

Remove any stems from the mallow leaves, then wash and chop them.

Put all the ingredients except the oil into a pan with a heavy base. Cover and simmer for 10 minutes, then uncover, stir, and simmer for a few more minutes with the lid off.

Take the pan off the heat, then stir the oil through.

Serve with cous-cous and a dollop of yoghurt, or on crusty bread with a sprinkle of crumbled feta.

NOTES

Makes enough for 4 people

SOW THISTLE

(Scientific name: Sonchus oleraceus)

Even though it's got 'thistle' in its name, sow thistle doesn't have any painful prickles on it. It's actually very soft. Even though it's got 'sow' (which means a lady pig) in its name, it doesn't have trotters, ears, or a wiggly tail. Pigs and other animals do love to eat it though, so that's probably where it got its name.

What To Look For

Sow thistle is a cousin of dandelion, and when it's young it can look a bit similar: its leaves are 'toothed' and also grow from a central point at ground level. However, sow thistle's leaves have a more bluey-green colour and the young leaves are rounded at the ends.

As the plant ages, it grows upwards with a central stalk—a trick that dandelion never manages. The leaves' ends also become pointier. Its yellow flowers look like smallish dandelion flowers, but they grow in clusters at the top and sides of the plant. The seeds also have tiny blow-away umbrellas arranged in a ball like dandelion does, but the ball is smaller and a bit messier.

When you break off a piece of sow thistle you'll find it has a hollow stem. Sometimes it comes off with a quiet 'pop'. A circle of sticky white sap always forms on the ring of the broken stem.

Where To Look

Sow thistle is *everywhere*. You'd be forgiven for thinking it was following you around. In summer and autumn you may need to look in slightly shadier or wetter areas for the best ones.

When To Look

All year round, but it's often tastiest in winter and spring.

milky sap on a broken stalk

How To Pick And Prepare It

You can pick the young leaves and eat them raw. Mostly you'll find the plant when it's older and growing strongly upwards. In that case, you pick the growing tips. Each one will contain a few leaves and maybe even some flower buds. If the tips are fresh and green and pop off nicely they'll be good eating. If the flowers have already turned into seeds, you're a bit too late. Look out for aphids — tiny, tiny insects that drink the sap of the plant — sometimes there'll be whole little villages of them! They probably don't want to be eaten, and luckily for them, you probably don't want to eat them either.

How To Use It

The really young leaves can be used in salads and sandwiches just like lettuce. The growth tips from older plants need to be cooked to get rid of the bitterness. How? Well, you can steam them, stew them, simmer, or sauté them, blanch them, bake them, boil, or braise them. Did we mention frying? In Aotearoa (New Zealand), sow thistle is called by its Māori name, puha, and is a popular vegetable. It is often cooked with pork or other rich meats. One of our favourite methods is to simply cook the growth tips in a pan with a little olive oil for a couple of minutes, and then add a squeeze of lemon juice and a pinch of salt.

leaves get toothier as the plant gets older

In the stories of ancient Greece, there was a hero called Theseus who fought a half-human half-bull creature called the Minotaur. The Minotaur not only had a bull's head, but also ate bulls' heads for breakfast! On the way to the fight, Theseus ate a bowl of sow thistle for strength. And—spoiler alert—he won!

young plants like this are the best for using raw

The Gurnaikurnai people of what is now known as Gippsland in Victoria traditionally eat a plant that is a close relative to sow thistle. They believe that when they die, their spirits go to the land of this plant.

SCIENTIFIC NAMES

All plants have both a common name, like 'sow thistle', and a scientific name, like '*Sonchus oleraceus*'. Don't worry too much about how to say scientific names. People might *say* them a bit differently, but they always *spell* them the same.

The same plant can have three, ten, or even more common names. For example, many people call sow thistle 'milk thistle'. But there are several *other* plants called 'milk thistle' too! Some of them you can eat and some of them you can't. There's only ONE plant called *Sonchus oleraceus* though, and you can definitely eat it. So there is a kind of power in knowing the scientific name—you always know exactly which plant you're talking about.

Just like common names, scientific names often describe something about the plant. In sow thistle's case, *Sonchus* means 'hollow', which describes the plant's hollow stem. *Oleraceus* means 'good to eat'. Purslane's scientific name contains a similar word, '*oleracea*', which means the same thing. The '*Stellaria*' part of chickweed's scientific name means 'star' and describes the plant's star-shaped white flowers.

All these meanings come from ancient languages like Latin, which people haven't spoken for thousands of years. Many of the spells from Harry Potter are also written in Latin! Come to think of it, while it's good to know scientific names, perhaps be cautious about saying them out loud under a full moon while holding wand-shaped twigs—you never know exactly what might happen...

WILD LETTUCE

(Scientific name: Lactuca serriola)

Lettuce comes in many types. But once upon a time there was really only one type of lettuce. And it was the great, great, great, great, great, great (add another 4,000 'greats') grandmother lettuce. Instead of growing on farms and in gardens it was more of an outlaw lettuce. It grew wherever it wanted – at least, at first. Then, thousands of years ago, some farmers started telling it where to grow. They chose the baby lettuces that they liked and kept the seeds from those ones to plant. Over the years they changed its shape and colour and made all the types of lettuce we have today. You might think that was the end of the story for the outlaw-grandmother lettuce, but no! Her untamed grandchildren – we call them wild lettuce – are still around! And if you know how, you can still find them ... and eat them.

What To Look For

Wild lettuce has narrower leaves than the kinds of lettuce that you grow in the garden or buy at the shops. In fact, when it's young its leaves aren't that different to dandelion leaves. They are a light, bright green and have serrated edges ('serrated' means shaped like the edge of a saw). As they get older these leaves develop big tooth shapes along their edges and turn a teensy bit blue.

Wild lettuce is also known as 'prickly lettuce'. When it's young and fresh, it has a single row of pale hairs running along the underside of each leaf, right down the middle. When it gets older, that line of hairs turns into a line of dark prickles! Looking for this row of hairs is one of the main ways to recognise wild lettuce. Also, when you pick it you might see some white sap in the cut.

this leaf is upside down so you can see the rows of hairs

Wild lettuce leaves grow out from a central point at ground level when the plant is young. And then, just like sow thistle (page 22), it starts forming a main stalk and growing upwards. That's when its leaves begin to get toothy and grow those dark prickles we talked about. Sometimes it grows prickles on its stalk, too. It also gets *very* bitter, so it's only nice to eat when it's young. Towards the end of its life it makes little yellow flowers, which turn into seed heads that are fluffy like dandelion's, but smaller.

Where To Look

Wild lettuce likes sun, but doesn't mind a bit of shade. You'll find it in most of Australia, from Hobart to Alice Springs, but not right up in the tropics.

The ancient Egyptians really liked lettuce. They were the first to tame wild lettuce and they even held big parties on their farms for their god Min, who they thought had created the plant.

When To Look

All year round, but you'll mostly find it in its young and tasty form in winter or early spring.

How To Pick And Prepare It

Pick nice-looking leaves from young plants. Easy!

tasty young leaves

How To Use It

The leaves can be used in salads and sandwiches, just like, um…lettuce. Really, it tastes just like lettuce. Why? Because it *is* lettuce! We almost always use this as a salad green, or raw in other ways. But you can cook with it too. Try popping it in a soup or stir-fry towards the end of the cooking.

In some old English legends, eagles plucked wild lettuce and put its juice in their eyes to give them the power to see further! Unless you're an eagle, please don't try this at home.

these are definitely too old and bitter to eat

MAKE A LEAF LIBRARY

Botanists are people who study plants. Often they crawl around in bushes and through jungles collecting leaves, flowers, and seeds. They look very closely at these bits of plants and learn as much as they can from them.

Be a weed botanist! Collect a few leaves from your favourite weeds and trace around them on this page or on another sheet of paper. Fill in any veins or other features you can see—use different thicknesses of pencil to show the different-sized veins. We've done one to get you started.

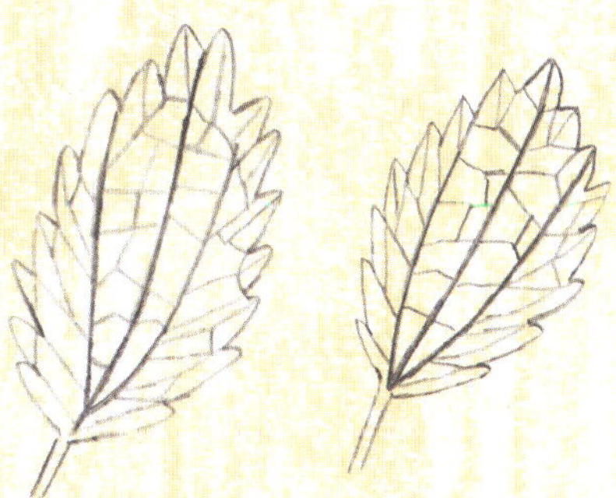

NETTLE LEAF

WEED NAME: ________________

DATE: ______________________

LOCATION FORAGED: __________

____

ANGLED ONION

(Scientific name: *Allium triquetrum*)

Angled onion looks like a pretty bunch of fairytale flowers, but smells like garlic bread—which is confusing, but also delightful! No prizes for guessing that it is in the same family as onion, leek, spring onion, and garlic. Well, just one prize: you get to eat yummy angled onion.

What To Look For

Before it grows flowers, angled onion looks a lot like super-enthusiastic grass. Grass that is bright green and about as tall as a short quokka—that's about 40 centimetres for those of you who don't live in a quokka colony. Peer a little closer and you'll notice that these leaves are thicker and fleshier than grass leaves. Cut one in half and you'll see the triangle shape that gives this plant the first part of its name. Pull one up and you'll see the stalk swell to form a small white bulb.

At this point you're also certain to smell the oniony scent that gives the plant the *other* part of its name. In fact, the best way to 'look' for angled onion can be to 'smell' for it! If you're out for a walk and you get a whiff of raw onions, chances are you're walking past a patch of angled onion.

The white flowers form in a group at the top of a stalk that grows a tiny bit taller than the leaves around it. They droop downwards like shy trumpets. Turn one up to face you and you'll see that the trumpet has six pointed petals.

Where To Look

If you offered an angled onion plant a pair of gumboots it would say, 'No thank you, I adore having wet toes.' So look in moist places in your garden, or near a creek or river if you know it's a nice clean one. It is very common in the southern states of

the flower stalks are even more triangular than the leaves

Australia, but not in the north — it's even pretty hard to find in New South Wales.

When To Look

You can find leaves from late autumn until early spring, but you'll have to wait until late winter for the flowers.

How To Pick And Prepare It

If you want your angled onion to grow back again, cut the leaves off just above the soil. If you'd like to eat the white part that grows underground (or to get rid of the plant because it's growing somewhere you don't want it to) pull the whole thing up. Give it a wash, chop the leaves into smallish bits, and you're ready to go!

The easiest way to harvest the flowers is to snip off a whole cluster and then pluck each flower off its little stem once you're in the kitchen. You can eat the big stalk that the flower cluster grows on too.

How To Use It

Anything that would taste good with spring onion will taste good with angled onion. The bonus is that maybe your grown-ups decide to give you extra pocket money because you saved them the bother of buying spring onions AND did some weeding (even if it was just by picking lunch).

Angled onion is better raw than cooked, although if you chop it finely it is perfect in omelettes or other foods that you don't cook for very long. The flowers are just as garlicky-oniony-tasting as the leaves, but with a sweetness that makes them our favourite bits. Try the leaves (including the white underground parts if you picked those) and flowers in a potato salad, a green salad, or mixed into a savoury, cheesy pancake or pikelet — check out the recipe on the next page.

Angled onion seeds may not have thumbs, but they are surprisingly good at hitchhiking. The plant attaches a little drop of oil to every seed. Ants think this oil is delicious, and carry the seeds away so that they can eat them. Then they leave the seeds lying about and baby angled onions pop up in new places.

People used to think garlic protected them from vampires. But leeches *prefer* skin that smells like garlic! So if you find yourself constantly being attacked by hordes of leeches, we suggest that you stop eating so much angled onion.

ANGLED ONION PIKELETS

INGREDIENTS

1 ½ cups plain flour
(gluten-free flour works too)
1 teaspoon baking powder
1 teaspoon bicarb soda
½ teaspoon salt
Big pinch of pepper
1 cup milk (cow or non-dairy)
1 tablespoon apple cider vinegar
or white vinegar
2 eggs
2 tablespoons olive oil
1 cup grated cheddar
(or 3 tablespoons nutritional yeast)
1 cup angled onion flowers
½ cup finely chopped angled onion
leaves (lower half of stalk only)
Butter or oil for frying

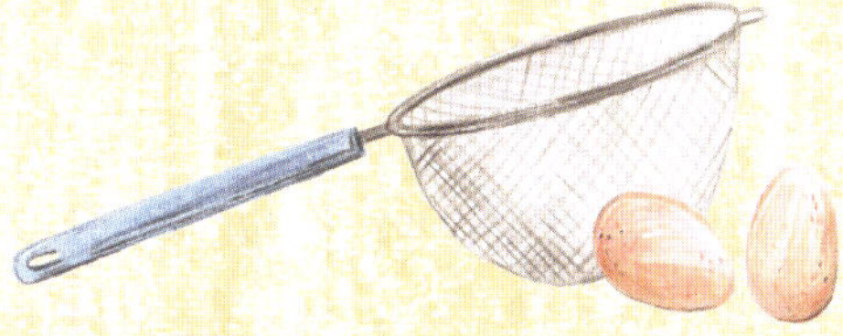

NOTES

Makes about 16 pikelets

The pikelets are just as delicious cold as they are hot, and they freeze well too.

DIRECTIONS

Sift the flour, baking powder, bicarb soda, salt, and pepper into a bowl.

In a separate bowl, add the vinegar to the milk to sour it. Wait for a few minutes, then if it doesn't curdle, add a tiny bit more vinegar.

Beat the eggs and the olive oil into the soured milk.

Add the milk mixture to the dry ingredients and stir until any lumps are gone.

Stir in the grated cheese.

Melt some butter in a pan and drop large spoonfuls of the mixture into it.

Sprinkle as many angled onion flowers and chopped leaves onto the top of each pikelet as you can fit!

Wait for each pikelet to puff up and form little bubbles on its surface, then flip it over to finish cooking.

FAT HEN

(Scientific name: Chenopodium album)

Despite its name, this weed is a great one to know even if you're not a chicken trying to put on weight. It has a lovely mild taste and you can quickly pick quite a lot if you find a good plant. It's also packed with protein.

What To Look For

One of fat hen's other names is 'goosefoot', because the shape of its leaves reminded some people in olden-day England of a goose's foot. They also thought that fat hen was pretty tasty — they planted it and grew it in their fields just like farmers do these days with spinach.

These 'goosefoot' leaves grow on thin stems branching off a thicker stalk that comes up from the ground. They are a dull green on top. On the side that faces downwards, they have a white dusty coating. The stems and leaves near the tips of each branch are covered in the same white coating, making it look like they have been dunked in icing sugar.

Fat hen is certainly not a show-off when it comes to making flowers. They appear in late summer and look a lot like tiny balls of pale-green belly-button fluff clustered at the end of each stem. You would need a magnifying glass to see them properly. Later on, they turn a bit red and make zillions of little shiny black seeds.

Most fat hen plants get about as tall as a kid's armpit, but a really happy one can get taller.

Where To Look

You can find fat hen growing in sunny spots in every state in Australia. It often pops up where someone has been digging or moving the soil around. This is because seeds that have been hanging out underground get

young growth looks whitish and a little sparkly

moved up near the sunlight and suddenly get the brilliant idea to start growing.

When To Look

Late spring and summer in the colder states of Australia, but year-round in the warmer ones. If it's warm enough for ice cream to melt down your wrist from the ice cream cone you're holding, it's warm enough for fat hen to grow!

How To Pick And Prepare It

Pick the younger leaves, which are the ones growing towards the top and outside of the plant.

Fat hen contains oxalic acid, which you can read some information about on page 5. Because of this, if you're eating more than a handful, you should quickly simmer the leaves in hot water, and then drain the water away. Then they will be ready to eat or add to other dishes.

How To Use It

Fat hen's gentle flavour means you can use it anywhere you would use spinach. It even has a silky texture a lot like spinach. Put it in a quiche or a vegetable soup. In India it's known as *bathua* and is the star of a popular curry called *bathua ka saag*.

How about fat hen savoury French toast? Chop up a handful of fat hen and mix it with milk and beaten eggs, then soak some stale bread in this mixture. Gently fry your soggy bread until all the egg is cooked, then put slices of tomato on top. Then put it in your tummy (via your mouth, of course).

Archaeologists in Denmark were very excited when they found a 1,700-year-old mummified man in a bog. They were even more excited when they realised that the bog had preserved the man perfectly—it was even possible to tell what he had been eating by looking in his stomach! And some of the things he'd been eating were fat hen seeds.

SAVING THE WORLD, ONE SALAD AT A TIME

Unfortunately, producing food these days uses a lot of resources. Even growing something simple like a lettuce probably uses more resources than you would guess. Water gets pumped out of rivers to put on the fields, and chemical fertilisers and insecticides are mined from the ground or made in factories. After the lettuces are grown, trucks use fuel to get them to shops, and shops use electricity to keep them cold until you buy them.

Sadly, using all of these resources creates pollution and damages the homes of the animals, fish, and birds that live in our environment. Sometimes they get sick from the chemicals or from not having clean water to drink or swim in.

The amazing thing about edible weeds is that no chemicals, truck fuel, or river water are used to grow them. They just grow themselves!

So next time you sit down to tuck into a weed salad, look deep into its fresh, crunchy leaves and whisper, 'You're probably the most environmentally friendly thing I've ever eaten.'

Just don't expect it to answer back. It is a salad, after all.

CHEESE 'N' WEEDS PIE (HORTOPITA)

INGREDIENTS

7 sheets filo pastry
½ cup extra virgin olive oil
250 grams (about six cups squashed down) fresh weeds such as dandelion, fat hen, mallow, nettle, and sow thistle
2 cups oxalis leaves if in season (or add a tablespoon of lemon juice and a teaspoon of lemon zest to the greens while they are cooking)
4 tablespoons finely chopped dill or mint
2 medium onions
2 eggs
160 grams crumbled Greek feta
250 grams ricotta
1 tablespoon grated parmesan
Salt and pepper
1–2 teaspoons sesame seeds or poppy seeds

NOTES

Makes 6 small slices

This recipe is for a small pie. If you want leftovers, double the quantities and use a bigger baking dish that can roughly fit a whole sheet of filo pastry.

DIRECTIONS

Move the filo pastry from the freezer to the fridge to thaw while you're making the filling.

Heat a tablespoon of the olive oil in a big pot on low heat and fry the onions until soft. Move to a !arge bowl and leave to cool.

Wash all the greens (including the dill or mint and oxalis) and pat dry with a tea towel. Chop them really well, making sure to cut *across* the leaves.

Put the weeds into the pan that the onion was cooked in and stir continuously over a low heat until they are wilted and any liquid has evaporated. Place them in a colander and let them drain.

Preheat your oven to 180°C.

Add the eggs to the bowl containing the onions and beat them with a fork. Then mix in the feta, ricotta, parmesan, salt, and pepper.

Squeeze the greens with your hands to get all the liquid out, then add to the egg-and-cheese bowl. Mix it all together.

Brush a baking dish with olive oil. You can use a round pie dish or a tin that is about 20 by 20 centimetres.

Take out seven sheets of filo pastry and cut them in half. Place a half sheet in the baking dish. Scrunch it a bit to make it fit—this makes the pie even yummier. Keep adding half sheets of pastry, brushing lots of oil onto each sheet as you go. Stop when you have seven sheets.

CHEESE 'N' WEEDS PIE (HORTOPITA)

DIRECTIONS CONTINUED

Empty the weeds mixture into the baking dish and spread it evenly over the pastry.

Cover the filling with seven more layers of filo pastry, brushing each sheet with olive oil. After placing the last pastry sheet, brush it with oil, and sprinkle it with a little bit of water and the sesame or poppy seeds.

Using a knife, cut partly into the top pastry layers to mark out six pieces. Don't cut all the way through!

Bake in the bottom half of the oven for about 50 minutes.

Have you identified, picked, and eaten at least three of the plants in this book so far? If the answer is yes, congratulations! You've earned your Advanced Forager's Licence!
ADVANCED FORAGER'S LICENCE
AWARDED TO:
LET'S EAT WEEDS!
DATE
SIGNATURE

The weeds that appear in this book after this page are some of our favourite weeds to eat. They also all have something a little bit tricky about them: cheeky prickles or spiky spines, toxic parts that you need to avoid, or similar-looking plants that can be dangerous.

That's not as scary as it might sound. Millions of people all over the world eat these plants regularly and are happier and healthier because of it! That's because those people already know the stuff that we're about to tell you in this book.

For every plant you'll find a **'Careful-ometer'**. This is where you can check how careful you need to be and why. **Use your Advanced Forager's powers wisely and ask an adult if you're unsure about anything.** Adults don't always know more than you do, but they are usually very good at looking things up.

GALLANT SOLDIER

(Scientific name: Galinsoga parviflora)

You know how soldiers wear camouflaged clothing so that they're hard to see when they're hiding among plants? Well this soldier has the best *camouflage of all. It actually* is *a plant!*

What To Look For

Gallant soldier grows upright, to about the height of a kid's waist. The thin green stems branch out and grow lots of pointy bright-green leaves. These leaves are never lonely because they always grow in pairs across from each other.

The main thing to look out for though, is its strange little flowers. They have tiny white petals around a yellow centre. Each petal has three 'teeth' at the end. The petals have gaps between them, almost like there used to be more of them—until a fussy petal-burglar picked off every second one under the cover of night. The flowers turn into a small ball of fluffy seeds.

Where To Look

This weed loves warmer weather, and you'll find it up in the tropical parts of Australia. But it will grow in the colder states, even if it's a bit grumpy about it. It's quite rare in Victoria and Tasmania, so if you spot a gallant soldier in those states you should be proud! It probably won't be in faraway bush, but in a crack in some concrete or near a road, soaking up the heat. It grows in full sun or partial shade and prefers moist soil.

CAREFUL-OMETER

Reasons For Being Careful

Gallant soldier has some similar-looking cousins. A couple of these are mildly toxic when eaten raw (although some people do eat them cooked). These plants include:

- Coat-buttons (scientific name: *Tridax procumbens*), which grows shorter than gallant soldier, except for its long flower stems. It only grows in Queensland and the hotter parts of Australia.
- St Paul's wort (scientific name: *Sigesbeckia orientalis*), which has yellow petals and five weird sticky little green 'fingers' behind the flowers.

How To Be Careful

Like always, you must—you must!—make sure you have the right plant.

When To Look

All year round, but if you live somewhere with frosty winters then you'll find it mostly in the warmer months.

How To Pick And Prepare It

Pick off the young growth tips including their leaves. Remove any flowers or larger flower buds.

How To Use It

Gallant soldier has a nice mild taste with no bitterness. Some people say it tastes a little like artichokes or parsnip. Even if you don't like these vegetables, we think you might like this plant. We eat it in salads or cooked. In Colombia, where it is native, it's known as *guasca* and it's the main herb in a potato soup called *ajiaco*. You can also dry it and use it as flavouring in soups and stews.

Gallant soldier's scientific name is *Galinsoga parviflora*. When people heard the word 'Galinsoga' some of them thought they were hearing 'gallant soldier' and started calling the plant by that name instead—and it stuck. In London, some kids have started calling it 'gallon of soda' for the same reason. Try saying it out loud yourself!

Have you ever gone for a walk only to get home and discover that you have long black seeds stuck all over your shoelaces and socks? You may have just met cobbler's pegs (scientific name: *Bidens pilosa*). It's another cousin of gallant soldier and is also eaten as a green vegetable by many cultures.

HOW TO SQUASH FLOWERS

Have you ever found a flower that you loved so much, you wished it would last forever? We can't really help you there, but there is a way to enjoy looking at it for a very, very long time.

Take your beautiful blossom (or sprig of blossoms) and place it on top of a piece of absorbent paper, such as parchment or tissue paper. Open the heaviest book you can find and place the flower on top of the absorbent paper on an inside page. Lay another sheet of absorbent paper on top of the flower, and then close the book. Squish! If you think the book isn't heavy enough, put a stack of other books on top of it. Wait for about two weeks for the flower to completely dry out. You can stick your pressed flower onto a card to give to someone as a present. For an extra challenge, try pressing a little posy.

CHICKWEED

(Scientific name: Stellaria media)

If you have the tastebuds of a chicken you'll looove chickweed. If you have the tastebuds of half of all human beings you'll also love chickweed, and will say lots of lovely things about its tender texture and mild flavour. If you have the tastebuds of the other half of all human beings you will say, 'Chickweed? Tastes kind of like grass, if you ask me.' And then you will probably eat it anyway, because it's crammed full of vitamins, minerals, and protein—AND it's free.

What To Look For

Keep your eye out for a bright-green little plant that often grows alongside its brothers and sisters into a leafy green carpet—quite a tall carpet! It reaches five to 25 centimetres high. Its leaves are delicate and shaped like teardrops, and its stems have a peculiar 'string' running through their core that stretches like elastic if you pull it.

It grows fuzzy little flower buds starting in midwinter, followed by small white flowers. Each flower has five bunny-eared petals (so it almost looks like there are *ten* teeny petals).

a chickweed flower with five 'bunny ear' petals

CAREFUL -OMETER

Reasons For Being Careful

There is a common plant that you could get muddled with chickweed, and it often grows in similar places. It's called petty spurge (scientific name: *Euphorbia peplus*), and you don't want to eat it because when broken it oozes a sticky white sap that can burn your mouth—or your eyes. There are some other slightly toxic plants that look a bit like chickweed too. None of them have the row of tiny hairs or the same kind of flowers.

How To Be Careful

Check that there is a mini-mohawk along the stem and NO white sap.

Top identification tip? Chickweed has a line of little hairs like a mini-mohawk growing along one side of the stem, which none of its look-alikes have. IMPORTANT identification tip? Chickweed has no white sap, whereas its inedible look-alike, petty spurge, does. Check out the Careful-ometer for more on petty spurge.

Where To Look

Your veggie patch or the tops of plant pots are good places to start. Or anywhere with nice, rich, moist soil. Chickweed grows in every state in Australia, but isn't very common in the tropics.

When To Look

The cooler, rainier months of the year. It can last into early summer in a moist, shady spot.

How To Pick And Prepare It

Find a nice, lush patch of chickweed — no problem if it has flowers or flower buds on it as they're tasty too. Pretend it's hair. Use some scissors to chop the top five centimetres off that 'hair' into a bowl. Give it a wash — *not* with shampoo! It's not *really* hair. Then pat it gently dry with a tea towel and chop it *across* the stems into pieces no more than two centimetres long. Any bigger and you'll get bits of that stretchy core stuck between your teeth like a swamp monster.

How To Use It

Chickweed is perfect for mixing with more strongly flavoured weeds like dandelion, sow thistle, and oxalis. Imagine that dandelion is a velociraptor and chickweed is a gentle baby brontosaurus: you obviously need both to make a well-rounded salad.

Chickweed is best eaten raw. Put it in a sandwich, a wrap, or anywhere else you might use lettuce. One of our favourite ways to eat it is in a brown rice or quinoa salad. Use about one cup of cooked, cooled brown rice or quinoa with one cup of chickweed and one cup of any of the following: capsicum, celery, apple, roast pumpkin…or use your imagination. Sprinkle with a handful of nuts, seeds, or feta and mix it all together with some yummo dressing.

Chickweed contains more than twice as much iron as spinach!

In the mythology of the Ainu people of Japan, the first people on earth had spines made from willow sticks and hair made of chickweed.

stretchy string inside stem

CHICKWEED PESTO

INGREDIENTS

3 cups tightly packed chickweed tops
¾ cup raw cashews
3 cloves garlic
1 tablespoon apple cider vinegar
1 tablespoon lemon juice
¼ cup extra virgin olive oil
Salt to taste — probably about ½ tsp
Pepper

NOTES

Makes about 1 ½ cups

DIRECTIONS

Chop your chickweed across the stem so that it ends up in pieces no more than two centimeters long.

Put one cup of the chickweed into a food processor (or blender if you don't have one) along with the oil, vinegar, and lemon juice. Add about a tablespoon of water and blend until all the leaves are finely chopped (but not until smooth). If it's not happening easily, gradually add a little more water or oil.

Tip: If you're using a blender, you'll need to stop it every few seconds, take the lid off, and give everything a stir. This stops you ending up with puree on the bottom and unblended leaves sitting on top.

Add the garlic and the cashews, then give the blender or food processor a few pulses until they break up very roughly. Add the rest of the chickweed and the salt and pepper.

Blend until all the chickweed is broken down, but stop while you still have a nice chunky pesto. If it still won't blend, add a dash more of whichever of the liquids your tastebuds tell you is missing.

NETTLE

(Scientific name: Urtica urens)

It's the 'ouch' that gives this weed away. If you've just touched a plant that seems to think it's a nest full of angry ants, it's probably nettle. Don't get mad – get even! Learning how to eat nettles is definitely the most delicious way to get your revenge.

What To Look For

Nettle *looks* sweet and innocent enough. It stands up proud and tall, growing to somewhere between the height of a chicken and the height of your kitchen table (depending on how much it likes where it's growing).

Bold green leaves grow on stems that come out on opposite sides of a main stalk. Each of those charming leaves has little teeth zigzagging around its edge… tipped with vicious stinging hairs! In fact, the whole leaf is covered in these hairs and so are the stems.

Nettle makes teeny-weeny flowers that you probably won't even notice. But you will see lots of small, round green seeds clustered along the stem and at the tip of each branch.

Where To Look

Nettle's favourite place to grow is a slightly shady spot with rich soil. But like many weeds, it likes to mix things up, so don't be surprised to see it enjoying sunny spots too. It does grow in every state of Australia, but you will find it much more often in the southern states.

CAREFUL -OMETER

Reasons For Being Careful

Nettle is covered in tiny stinging hairs. They can leave the bit of you that touched those hairs with a red prickly rash for an hour or two.

How To Be Careful

Use gloves and scissors to harvest, and disarm the sting with heat or by blending or drying.

When To Look

Mainly in the cooler months. Some really enthusiastic nettles keep growing right into summer though.

How To Pick And Prepare It

Hunting the wild nettle means becoming a foraging warrior. You need to respect the weapons of your target and use knowledge to avoid them.

Secret knowledge item 1: scissors, a bowl, and a glove.

A rubber washing-up glove will do. Put the glove on the opposite hand from the one you will use to hold the scissors. Use your gloved hand to hold the nettle stalk above the bowl. Chop off the growing tips and as many fresh-looking leaves as you want so that they drop into the bowl. Don't include too much stalk because nettle stalk is very stringy.

Secret knowledge item 2: heat.

In the kitchen, pour boiling water into your bowl of nettles. Stir them for a few seconds and *voila*! Harmless nettles. Move them quickly into a bowl of cold water if you'd like them to keep their bright-green colour.

It's the extreme heat that disarms the nettles, so you could also use this method: put on the second glove and use your gloved hands to chop the nettles and throw them into whatever you're cooking.

Secret knowledge item 3: pulverising!
If you want to eat your nettles raw, this method is for you. Blend your nettles into a green smoothie (like the one we have a recipe for on page 53). You could also whizz them up into a soup. Either way, the sting will magically disappear.

Even more magical, you can use the power of pulverising to let you pick and eat nettle leaves WITH YOUR BARE HANDS! Occasionally you might get a little sting, but if you're prepared to take that risk, here's how it's done: firmly pinch a nettle leaf from the underside so that it folds together; give it a little yank so that it comes off the plant; roll the leaf back and forth tightly between your fingers—then (gasp!) pop it into your mouth. There. Now take a bow and wait for the applause.

How To Use It

You can use nettle instead of spinach or silverbeet in any cooked dish. You can put it in a stew, minestrone, or curry, and it's very nice inside ravioli or made into gnocchi. Some people dry it to make tea.

If you happen to live in Dorset, England, you can enter the Annual World Nettle Eating Championship. You won't be cooking delicious recipes for this competition though—you have to eat your nettle raw. The winner is the person who eats the most in one hour!

Ever since ancient Roman times some people have used nettles in a rather surprising way: for whipping themselves with! It sounds crazy, but these people had arthritis and would treat their sore joints by hitting them with nettle plants. Even crazier? There's scientific evidence that it works!

Nettles are packed with vitamins and minerals, especially calcium. Eating just one good helping gives your body all the calcium it needs for that day.

GREEN SMOOTHIE

INGREDIENTS

1 medium banana (fresh or frozen)

1 medium orange or half a mango

1 cup water

½ to 1 cup (depending on how powerful you'd like your smoothie to be) of mixed weeds. Dandelion, sow thistle, chickweed, nettle, and mallow all work well.

NOTES

Makes enough to fill 2 or 3 big glasses

DIRECTIONS

Wash all the weeds and chop them up a bit—remove any thick stems first.

Peel and slice your orange, getting rid of any pips. Break the banana into chunks.

Plop all the ingredients into the blender and blend them until smooth and frothy. Done!

This is just a basic recipe. Use your imagination and add avocado, frozen berries... or whatever you like.*

*Don't add:

+ Fennel or too much purslane as their strong flavours will take over
+ Green crayons (or any other colour)
+ Hair (gross!)
+ Noodles (too noodly)
+ Library books (you could get a fine)
+ Tears of a walrus (too salty)

BLACKBERRY

(Scientific name: Rubus fruticosus)

It scritches and scratches, it grows in thorny patches! Which is why this weed is definitely one for the Advanced Forager. Personally, we think that the adventure of collecting blackberries makes them taste even more delicious than they already are – which is pretty darn delicious.

What To Look For

Blackberry grows on long, wild stalks called canes that shoot up out of the ground and make a big, crazy tangle – a bit like a gigantic hairball, but spiky. Or like a raspberry plant that forgot to stop growing. The canes can grow as thick as your thumb, and one patch could fill your entire classroom... if your classroom had soil instead of a floor... and you took off the roof to let sunlight and rain in.

Blackberry leaves are dark green and dull rather than shiny. Their edges have tiny zigzag shapes. In spring and summer, pretty white flowers with five petals appear. These become the fruit, which starts green and then turns red. You don't want to eat them like that because they are hard and sour and will give you quite a bellyache. But don't worry: the magicky magic of summer will slowly transform those red berries into sweet and juicy black ones. When you smoosh these ripe berries they smear purple juice all over whatever they touch. In long-ago times people used this juice as lipstick. Try it for yourself!

CAREFUL -OMETER

Reasons For Being Careful

You can turn into a human pincushion with all those thorns about.

How To Be Careful

Wear a sturdy outfit and bring on the tools! Use a walking stick to hook the canes towards you, or drop an old plank of wood onto the patch to use as a walkway to reach more berries.

Where To Look

Unlike many of the other weeds in this book you usually won't find blackberry hanging out in your local park. It really likes moist places — look near creeks or rivers. If you're in the countryside you might also find it growing in gullies or paddocks.

Although blackberry prefers cooler climates, it can be found in every state of Australia except the Northern Territory.

When To Look

Summer is the season for gobbling blackberries. You can find fruit in autumn too, but beware! Autumn blackberries can get mouldy inside, so if they taste a bit funny, spit them out. They won't turn you into a pumpkin or anything horrible like that, but they might have you sitting on the toilet more often than you'd like…

How To Pick And Prepare It

Imagine you go out for a walk and you pass a blackberry patch covered in lovely ripe fruit. You've already asked the grown-ups in your life to find out if the blackberries in your area have been sprayed this summer (see page 5 for some information on spraying). They made some phone calls, and the answer was 'no'. You're in luck! So you reach out to pick a couple of plump berries and pop them in your mouth. They are so scrumptious that you can't resist picking another handful...then another handful, and—oops! You've gotten hooked on a thorny cane, AND you're wearing your favourite T-shirt. Before you know it, you look like you've been wrestling with a very feeble tiger.

Do your grown-ups seem worried about you wrecking your clothes while picking blackberries? Try this little speech: 'Lovely grown-up, did you know that wild blackberries are incredibly high in antioxidants, manganese, and vitamin K, and they're FREE?' Grown-ups *love* antioxidants.

That's why we suggest choosing between the following outfits for blackberry picking: a) really old clothes, or b) really tough clothes—tight is better than baggy, because there's less to get snagged.

If there is a blackberry patch you visit regularly, you might want to make a path into the middle of it so that you can get in there to pick more berries. This mission really does need your toughest jeans. Or titanium trousers. Or a suit of armour. Starting from the edge, stomp the canes downwards with your foot until they are crushed to the ground. Work your way inwards. Then pick those berries until every finger is purple!

How To Use It

We mostly eat our blackberries fresh because they're so yummy that way. If you want to make something fancy, how about blackberry pie or crumble? Blackberry jam? Blackberry sauce to pour on yoghurt or ice cream, or to freeze into icy poles? See the recipe on the next page.

blackberry flowers and buds

BLACKBERRY SAUCE

INGREDIENTS

4 cups blackberries
3 tablespoons sugar
1 tablespoon lemon juice
1 teaspoon lemon zest
1 tablespoon cornflour
1 tablespoon water
Pinch of salt

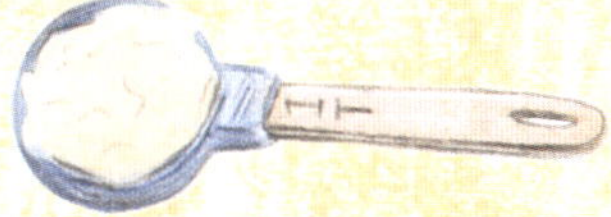

NOTES

Makes about 2 cups

DIRECTIONS

Bring the berries, sugar, salt, and water to a simmer while stirring constantly. Simmer for about five minutes.

Strain the seeds out by pushing the mixture through a big sieve (if you'd like a chunky sauce, only strain half the berries and leave the rest in the pot). Put your sieved juices back in the pot.

Mix the cornflour and lemon juice together in a small bowl. Make sure to get rid of ALL the lumps.

Gradually stir the cornflour mixture into the berry mixture.

Add the lemon zest. Bring your pot of berries to the boil, stirring all the while. Keep stirring it until it is thick – probably for a couple of minutes.

BLACKBERRY NIGHTSHADE

(Scientific names: Solanum nigrum and Solanum americanum)

We grew up calling this plant 'deadly nightshade', although that's not its proper name. But is it dangerous? Well, yes. And also no. Millions of people all around the world eat it and don't get sick. But you need to know how to eat it. This is also true of its cousins: potato, tomato, and eggplant. These plants can all be poisonous too, but we can learn to eat them safely. In fact, you probably already do.

What To Look For

Blackberry nightshade usually grows about as tall as a chair. It grows upwards and outwards, branching regularly with leaves that are a darkish green, sometimes with a hint of purple. The leaves are shaped like... well, leaves. Sometimes they have smooth edges and sometimes they are a bit rippled.

Its flowers are about one centimetre across and star-shaped. They have five triangular white petals and a yellow bit in the middle. The pea-sized berries start off green, then turn black when they ripen. They grow in clusters of about five to 12. Each berry is attached to the plant by what looks like a five-pointed green elf hat.

Where To Look

Blackberry nightshade likes all kinds of conditions, from full sun to part shade. It pops up in almost everyone's garden at one time or another.

CAREFUL-OMETER

Reasons For Being Careful

The unripe berries and possibly the leaves of some plants contain the same toxins as you find in green potatoes. They could make you sick if you ate too much. Blackberry nightshade also has some similar-looking relatives. Most of these are likely edible, but they haven't all been tested by science, so they're best left alone.

How To Be Careful

Don't eat big amounts at one time. Always boil the leaves and drain away the cooking water. If any berries or leaves taste bitter, don't eat them. If the plant looks a bit funny and you're not certain it's blackberry nightshade, don't pick it.

When To Look

Like its cousin the tomato, blackberry nightshade grows best in the warmer months. In colder parts of the country it mostly dies away in winter. The berries ripen and turn black in summer and autumn. You'll find the best leaves in spring.

How To Pick And Prepare It

When the berries are ripe you will be able to tug them gently and have them drop off the plant into your hand, leaving behind their elf hats. To harvest the leaves, choose healthy-looking younger growth.

How To Use It

Blackberry nightshade contains some toxins, which are mostly found in the green berries. Potatoes contain the exact same toxins, especially when they are green or sprouting. Luckily, these toxins don't taste very good. If you tried to eat those green berries, they'd be so bitter that you'd spit them out pretty fast! But when they turn black they are safe to eat, and super sweet and delicious — kind of like a cross between a blackcurrant and a tomato. We usually just eat a handful at a time fresh from the plant. Or sometimes we throw them into a salad — they are especially nice in a brown rice salad.

During the gold rush, blackberry nightshade was brought to Australia to be used as a leaf vegetable. In India they cook it with onion and spices like cumin. In Greece the leaves are called *istifno* and are sometimes cooked along with dandelion. People also eat them in Indonesia, Hawaii, Africa, and Turkey. Despite this popularity we don't eat the leaves very often — see the Careful-ometer for why.

Have you made something super scrumptious out of weeds? Here's your chance to be a published cookbook author! Write down your ingredients and what you did with them on a scrap piece of paper. When you've got it worked out, copy it onto the next page.

INGREDIENTS

DIRECTIONS

NOTES

PRICKLY PEAR

(Scientific name: Opuntia species)

Take one look at this spiky cactus and you'll know you've truly made it to the Advanced Forager's part of the book. You have to be very careful with this thorny food. It's been known to make grown adults cry. But it's one of our favourite weeds and we're not alone. In fact, ask ALL OF MEXICO, because that country loves it too. Their flag even shows an eagle eating a rattlesnake while perching on a prickly pear.

What To Look For

Prickly pear is made up of oval or round 'pads' all growing out of each other. Each pad is kind of flat, but also thick and fleshy like a cactus—which it is! The pads can be bigger than a person's head and are covered in bumps that look like pimples. Out of each bump grow *very* sharp thorns.

Fresh young pads are glossy and bright green. They turn dull green as they get older. The bottom of really old plants can grow into something like a round, brown tree trunk.

close-up of the tiny spines on the fruit—BEWARE!

CAREFUL -OMETER

Reasons For Being Careful

The pads have big spines that can spike you. The fruits have tiny, almost invisible spines that can get stuck in your skin and be *very* irritating.

How To Be Careful

Use gloves and the other equipment that we've described to help you harvest and prepare your lovely cactus lunch. Don't forget your grown-up helper.

The flowers are bright yellow or sometimes orange. They turn into fruit that is shaped like a big egg, or sometimes a bit like a pear. It starts out green then turns yellow, orange, pink, red, or purple when it gets ripe.

You might think the fruit doesn't look as tricky to pick as the pads, because it doesn't have big, scary spines. But it's actually *much* trickier. See the little bumps on the fruit? These are lots of small, hair-like spines that you can hardly see. These itchy tricksters can get stuck in your skin and are very hard to get out!

Prickly pear plants can grow twice as high as an adult. Unlike most of the other plants in this book, they live for many years.

Where To Look

Prickly pear grows all over Australia. You might find a patch next to a railway line, in a paddock, or in someone's backyard. Because it's a cactus, it can grow in hot and dry places.

When To Look

The young pads, which are good for eating, like to grow in spring and early summer. Picking these pads tricks the plant into growing more fresh pads so that you can eat them right into autumn — or year-round if you live somewhere warm in winter. The fruit ripens in autumn.

How To Pick And Prepare It

Okay, this is one plant that will require a grown-up to help you pick and prepare it. Choose the tallest adult you can find because the best fruits and pads are sometimes up high.

Gloves can help, but they aren't nearly enough! A pair of long tongs is best. You can pull off the ripe fruit with them. If you're collecting the pads you will need tongs *and* a knife. Look for those fresh, green young pads and cut them off right where they meet the pad below.

If you collect the fruit in a bag, use an old plastic bag that you can throw away afterwards because all the little hairs will be stuck in it. If you collect the fruit in a big bowl you can wash the bowl later.

Some people stick a fork in the fruit, being careful not to touch it, and burn the hairs off over a gas stove. Other people use a knife and fork to cut it open and a spoon to scoop out the tasty insides. Whichever way you choose, be careful to also not touch anything that the fruit has touched until you have washed it wearing rubber gloves. Those little hairs are hard to spot and spread faster than glitter at a sparkle party.

If you've collected the pads, you need an adult to 'shave' them. Here's what they should do: take a sharp knife and slide it over the surface of the pad, cutting all the bumps off (and with them, the spines). Do this on both sides, then cut around the edges. Keep gloves on while chucking out the spiny bits and washing off the chopping board and knife.

Birds — especially emus — once spread prickly pear plants all over Australia by eating them and pooping out the seeds. There was too much of it, so a beetle was introduced to Australia to eat it. This worked, and now there's less prickly pear growing wild.

How To Use It

Prickly pear fruit tastes a bit like strawberries and melon mixed together, but with quite big seeds. You can eat the fruit fresh, turn it into jam, or blend it into smoothies.

But wait, this wonderful weed is both fruit *and* vegetable! Once you've gotten rid of the spines you can barbeque whole pads of prickly pear, or just cook them in a sandwich press. We like to slice them up into strips the size of asparagus and fry them. You can cut them into pieces, then steam them, then add them to omelettes, pizza toppings, taco fillings, and stir fries. They are a bit... how do we say this? Slimy. But in a gooood way. They taste a bit like green beans with a hint of lemon.

In Mexican Spanish the pads of prickly pear are called *nopales*, and the fruit is called *tuna*! So if, one day, you are using a Mexican fruit salad recipe, be careful not to put tinned fish on it by mistake ...

how to prepare a pad for cooking

prickly pear flower

fruit can come in orange, red, and purple

FENNEL

(Scientific name: Foeniculum vulgare)

What can grow taller than a donkey and tastes like licorice? Wild fennel! This feathery plant is the lolly in the edible weeds corner store, so keep an eye out for it growing by a creek near you.

What To Look For

Like many plants, fennel looks different at different times of year. When it's young, it's bright green and about the same height as a table. The leaves are so thin that they look like threads. Because they grow very close together, a young fennel plant can look almost like a bunch of giant, green fluffy cats' tails.

When the plant gets older, the leaves space out more and you can see their 'thread' shape very easily. They also turn dull dark green. Tall stalks as thick as your finger sprout up from the centre of the plant. These are flower stalks, and each one branches out to grow many flowers. The flowers grow in an umbrella shape that can be as wide as your hand. Every 'umbrella' is actually lots of little stems holding up lots of teeny-tiny yellow flowers. As summer goes on these flowers will become the plant's seeds.

Where To Look

If plants could get a suntan, fennel would have one. It likes to grow in the hottest spot it can find. Next time you catch a train, look out the window and you might see fennel growing nearby—it loves how the rocks either side of the tracks soak up the sun's heat.

If sunshine is fennel's favourite thing, water is definitely its second favourite.

CAREFUL-OMETER

Reasons For Being Careful

Other plants have seed heads that look very similar to fennel's seed heads. One of those plants is hemlock (*Conium maculatum*), which is a very dangerous plant indeed.

How To Be Careful

Never collect seeds unless you can see the leaves to confirm that the plant is actually fennel.

Creeks and streams often have a few patches of fennel nearby, happily wiggling their roots down into the moist soil.

You can find fennel in every state of Australia except for the Northern Territory.

Some people use fennel seeds as medicine to treat…farts! This works because the plant contains special oils that help your stomach stay relaxed while it digests food.

When To Look

Look for fresh new leaves from early spring until summer. The flowers and seeds appear as things really heat up. In late summer fennel mostly shrivels up into dry brown stalks that not even a panda would want to chew. It stays that way all through winter.

How To Pick And Prepare It

If you buy fennel from a shop, it has a big round white bit at the bottom of the leaves called a 'bulb'. Wild fennel doesn't have a bulb, so which bits do you eat? You eat the leaves, seeds, and the pollen. The youngest leaves are the yummiest ones. These are bright, bright, light green and grow towards the middle of the plant.

Fancy a fennel pollen lollipop? When the flowers first come out, bend one down and give it a lick! Check for insects first, because they think that fennel pollen is delicious too.

When the flowers turn into seed heads, this is where your Advanced Forager's Licence comes in: NEVER pick the seeds from an old dry fennel plant whose leaves have all wilted and turned brown. If you can't see those thread-like leaves, you can't be sure it's fennel. One VERY poisonous plant called hemlock has seed heads that look a lot like fennel's seed heads, but its leaves look more like a carrot top, and its flowers are white not yellow.

While fennel's leaves are still green, the seeds are greenish yellow and a bit soft. We like to nibble on them whenever we pass a fine-looking fennel.

How To Use It

Fennel seeds and leaves have a sweet flavour a lot like licorice. Simply popping some into your mouth as you are walking along is a delicious, refreshing treat.

At home, try frying the seeds up with onion to make a cauliflower curry. Shazam! Chefs often cook fennel leaves or seeds with chicken or fish, especially in a cream sauce. You can also use the leaves in a salad.

Chewing on fennel seeds can also help to get rid of stinky breath. In medieval times, toothbrushes hadn't been invented yet, and it was common advice to 'cleanse your mouth with fennel' if you were hoping to kiss somebody!

1. Which weed in this book has a hollow stalk that oozes white sap, and a scientific name that means 'hollow and good to eat'?
2. Name two ways that you can disarm a nettle's sting.
3. What time of year do blackberries mostly ripen?
4. Which weed in this book contains more calcium per cup than milk does? Bonus points if you can name the other weed in the book that is super high in calcium.
5. What should you look for if you want to be certain that a plant is chickweed and not one of its look-alikes?
6. Which weed in this book has a white coating on the bottom side of its leaves and on its new growth?
7. Name a weed that has love-heart shaped leaves in threes and tastes like sucking on a lemon.
8. You're out for a walk and you see chickweed, nettle, and young wild lettuce. What season are you in?
9. Name a weed that could give you garlic breath, and a weed that can make your breath sweet.
10. If you ate weeds every day, would you get so healthy that your friends would throw you into a well out of jealousy?

(answers on the next page)

Thanks to the special people and wild places that raised us, and to all those kids whose enthusiasm for eating weeds made it so obvious that this book should exist. A special thanks to Richard Camilleri for much typing help.
—Annie Raser-Rowland & Adam Grubb

For Bronson: may you always be wild and free! Love, aunty Evie

The illustrations in this book were made with coloured pencils, pastels, and Procreate.
Typeset in Archer by Miriam Rosenbloom
Hand-lettering by Evie Barrow

Scribble, an imprint of Scribe Publications
18–20 Edward Street, Brunswick, Victoria 3056, Australia

Design by Miriam Rosenbloom

Published by Scribble 2021
Reprinted 2021

This book is printed with vegetable-soy based inks, on FSC® certified paper and other controlled material from responsibly managed forests, ensuring that the supply chain from forest to end-user is chain of custody certified. Printed and bound in China by 1010.

ISBN 978 1 922310 86 6 (Australian hardback)

Catalogue records for this title are available from the National Library of Australia.

scribblekidsbooks.com

The authors and publisher acknowledge the Wurundjeri Woi Wurrung of the Kulin Nations — the first and continuing custodians of the land on which this book has been created. Sovereignty has never been ceded. We pay our respects to Elders past and present. Both authors and publisher pledge to make regular financial contributions to First Nations-owned advocacy organisations.

ANSWERS: 1. Sow thistle. **2.** If you said any of these give yourself a tick: a) heating — in the form of boiling water or cooking; b) blending; c) drying; d) rolling the leaf between your fingers to crush the stinging hairs. **3.** Late summer. **4.** Mallow. And nettle is even higher in calcium! **5.** The line of tiny hairs along the stem. **6.** Fat hen. **7.** Oxalis (also give yourself a tick if you said 'sourgrass'). **8.** Probably winter. It could be spring or autumn, but it's very unlikely to be summer. **9.** Angled onion; fennel. **10.** It's a possibility.